The Three Little PIGS

RETOLD AND ILLUSTRATED BY
Barry Moser

Little, Brown and Company
Boston New York London

Once upon a time, when animals could talk the same as people, three little pigs lived with their mother in a forest.

It was Valentine's Day when Big Mama Pig said, "It's time for you to go out in the wide world to seek your fortune. But remember, beware of the big bad wolf."

Then she kissed them all around, and the three little pigs set out on their travels, each taking a different road.

The first little pig hadn't gone far before he met a man carrying a bundle of straw. "Please," asked the pig, "will you give me some
of that straw to build a house?"

"Certainly," replied the man, and he gave the pig a big bundle.

No sooner had the little pig finished the house than a wolf came along, knocked at the door, and said, "Little pig, little pig, let me in."

But the little pig just laughed and answered, "No, no, no, not by the hair of my chinny chin chin."

Then the wolf said loudly, "Then I'll huff and I'll puff and I'll blow your house in!"

So he huffed and he puffed, and he blew the house in, because it was only straw. Then the wolf ate up the little pig and didn't leave so much as the tip of his curly tail.

The second little pig also met a man, and this man was carrying a bundle of wood. "Please," said the pig politely, "will you give me some wood to build a house?"

The man agreed, and the piggy set to work building himself a
snug little house. It was scarcely finished when the wolf came along
and said, "Little pig, little pig, let me in."

"No, no, no, not by the hair of my chinny chin chin," answered
the pig.

"Then I'll huff and I'll puff and I'll blow your house in!" said
the wolf. So he huffed and he puffed, and he puffed and he huffed,
and at last he blew the house in and gobbled the little pig right up!

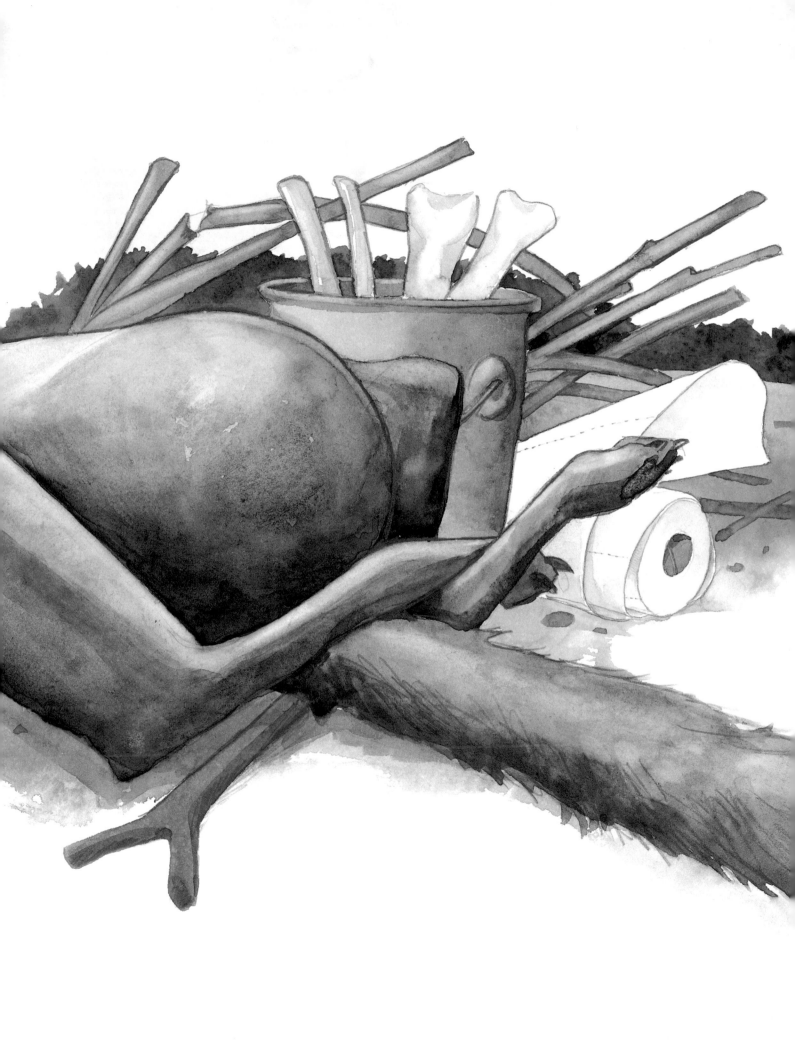

Now, the third little pig met a man with a load of bricks and said, "Please, may I have some bricks to build a house?"

The man agreed and also gave the pig some mortar and a trowel, and the little pig built himself a nice strong little house. As soon as it was finished, the wolf came to call, just as he had done to

the other little pigs, and said, "Little pig, little pig, let me in!"

But the little pig answered, "No, no, no, not by the hair of my chinny chin chin."

"Then," said the wolf, "I'll huff and I'll puff and I'll blow your house in!"

Well, the wolf huffed and he puffed, and he puffed and he huffed, and he huffed and he puffed, but he couldn't blow the house in. At last he had no breath left to huff and puff, so he sat down outside the little pig's house to think.

After a while the wolf called out, "Little pig, I know where there's a nice field of turnips."

"Where?" said the little pig.

"Behind the farmer's house, three fields away. I'll meet you here tomorrow morning at six o'clock, and we'll go there together and get some breakfast."

"All right," said the little pig, "I'll be ready."

Well, the smart little pig got up at five, scampered away to the

field, and brought home a fine load of turnips before the wolf came. At six o'clock the wolf came to the little pig's house and said, "Little pig, are you ready?"

"Ready?" cried the little pig. "I've been to the field and back long ago, and now I'm busy boiling a potful of turnips for breakfast."

Well, the wolf was very angry indeed, but he made up his mind to catch the little pig some way or another, so he told him that he knew where there was a nice apple tree.

"Where?" asked the little pig.

"Around the hill in the orchard," the wolf said. "If you promise not to play any more tricks, I'll meet you here tomorrow morning at five o'clock, and we'll go there and get some apples."

The next morning, the piggy got up at four o'clock and was gone long before the wolf came.

But the orchard was a long way off, and besides, he had the tree to climb, which is not an easy matter for a little pig, so before he had filled the sack he brought, he saw the wolf coming toward him.

The little pig was dreadfully afraid, but he thought it better to try to outsmart the wolf, so when the wolf said, "Little pig, why are you here before me? Are they nice apples?" he replied at once, "Yes, very; I'll throw one down for you to taste." So he picked an apple and threw it so far that while the wolf was running to fetch it, the

pig had time to jump down and scamper away home.

The next day the wolf came again and told the little pig that there was going to be a fair in the town that afternoon and asked him if he wanted to go together.

"Oh, yes," said the pig, "I'll go with pleasure. What time will you be ready to start?"

"At half past three," said the wolf.

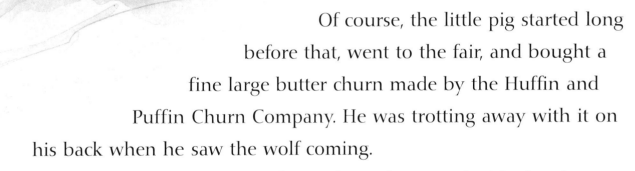

Of course, the little pig started long before that, went to the fair, and bought a fine large butter churn made by the Huffin and Puffin Churn Company. He was trotting away with it on his back when he saw the wolf coming.

He didn't know what else to do, so he crept inside the churn to hide. But the churn started rolling, and down the hill it went, rolling over and over, with the little pig squealing inside.

The wolf couldn't imagine what the strange thing rolling down the hill could be, so he turned tail in a fright and ran away home without going to the fair at all. Then he went to the little pig's house to tell him how scared he had been by a large round thing that came rolling past him down the hill.

"Ha, ha!" laughed the little pig. "So I scared you, eh? I'd been to the fair and bought a butter churn; when I saw you I got inside and rolled down the hill."

This made the wolf so angry that he declared he'd jump down the chimney and eat up the little pig!

But the clever little pig put a pot of water on the hearth and made a blazing fire. Just as the wolf was coming down the chimney, the pig took off the cover, and in fell the wolf. In a second the little pig had popped the lid on again.

The little pig had wolf stew for supper, and after that he lived happily all his days and was never troubled by a wolf again.

To the memory of my old friend
WILLIE MORRIS,
the only man I have ever known who could grasp
the gravity and true literary importance of this tale.

— B. M.

First Edition

Library of Congress Cataloging-in-Publication Data

Moser, Barry.
    The three little pigs / Barry Moser. – 1st ed.
      p. cm.
    Summary: A humorous retelling of the classic story recounts the fatal episodes in the
lives of two foolish pigs and how the third pig managed to avoid the same fate.
    ISBN 0-316-58544-0
    [1. Folklore. 2. Pigs – Folklore.] I. Title.

PZ8.1.M838 Th 2001
398.24'529633–dc21
[E]
                                           00-035228

10 9 8 7 6 5 4 3 2

TWP

Printed in Singapore

The illustrations for this book were done in watercolor on
Royal Watercolor Society paper.
The text was set in Nofret Regular.
The display type is handlettered.